If Love Be Lost - A Civil War Ladies' Story of Conflicted Loyalties

Monika L. Burkhart

Published by The Luminescent Paintbox, 2023.

This is a work of fiction. Similarities to real people, places, or events are entirely coincidental.

IF LOVE BE LOST - A CIVIL WAR LADIES' STORY OF CONFLICTED LOYALTIES

First edition. September 9, 2023.

ISBN: 979-8223722038

Written by Monika L. Burkhart.

Table of Contents

Prologue ~ St. Louis Divided

St. Louis Levee or Landing

This is a story of the American Civil War. But it is not about the men and their military pursuits. Rather, it is a story of the ladies they left behind.

It begins and ends in St. Louis, Missouri. The city played a key role in the conflict., as did some of it more famous inhabitants. William T. Sherman and Ulysses S. Grant lived there. Mrs. Elizabeth Keckley bought her freedom there. James B. Eads built his Union gunboats, there. And people were divided between the Confederacy and the Union, there.

You see, Missouri was a border state during the conflict, and its government sided with the South. Friends as well as families were separated by their sentiments. St. Louis was quickly placed in Union control, and for a period of time, the city was under Martial Law.

Women immediately, supported the cause in which they believed. Some participated in clandestine activities. One of those pursuits was delivering letters from men in the Southern army. If captured by Federal authorities, the woman could be imprisoned, or banished. And many a lady living in St. Louis during the Civil War had a secret tale or two, to tell.

Our chronicle begins at a small dress and millinery shop, at No. 132, Verandah Row. The proprietress is Miss Ginnie Allen, a young dressmaker, and according to the following conversation, is quite surely...a Yankee.

Verandah Row. St. Louis

Katie's eyes blazed with fiery indignation. "Holy angels, Cullie McCafferty," she fumed, as she arranged her millinery table. "If ya weren't me brother, I wouldn' say a single, syllable to ya, ever again!"

Cullie didn't retreat. Instead, he launched another volley. "Jumpin' Jiggers! If yer workin' fer Ginnie Allen—-then yer workin' fer a Yankee!"

"An' what if she is?" demanded Katie. "Miss Ginnie gives me six dollars a week. 'Tis a han'some wage fer a girl!"

Cullie pushed back his cap. "A tidy sum. An' maybe someday ya'll even, be worth it!"

Before Katie could take aim, the bell upon the shop door rang, and the proprietress entered the room. She placed a twine-tied package upon a shelf, and ignored Cullie, completely. He was there only to practice Base Ball at the park in the afternoon.

"Mornin', Miss Ginnie!" said Katie with a curtsy.

Ginnie removed her bonnet. "Good morning, Katie. Is Mrs. Brumley's order finished?"

A smile dimpled Katie's face. "It is, indeed!" A cloth was removed from a blue and white silk bonnet, liberally festooned with gaudy, red roses.

"Jumpin' jiggers...." winced Cullie.

Ginnie straightened her collar. "And what is Mrs. Brumley giving?"

"She's givin' ten dollars!" replied Katie, as she dusted the roses.

"Ten dollars?" Cullie retorted. "Fer that bit o' frippery?"

Ginnie gave Cullie a piercing glance. Why did men never understand the value of a bonnet?

"Mr. McCafferty...I am a business woman. My ambition is to accumulate as much money as possible. That head-wear sir, is my livelihood. And it is worth exactly ten dollars!"

Cullie crossed his arms. "Well, if it's money yer after...then, 'tis best yer robbin' a Yankee."

Ginnie caught her breath. Not so much for the presumption, but for one solitary, word: 'Yankee.' The dressmaker's family was from the east, and Ginnie was a Unionist at heart. Most of her patrons were ladies with Secessionist sympathies. Rebel sympathies. So she never spoke of her particular loyalty. Her shop, her work...all depended upon it. Ginnie Allen had to tread carefully. Very carefully.

Katie glowered at her older brother. "Cullen Patrick Aloysius McCafferty! You apologize dis very minute!"

The battle of words had been lost. "Well then," ventured Cullie, " 'tis sorry I am, fer sayin' what I shouldn' ta said."

"There is no harm done," replied Ginnie. "Perhaps a few manners might wear away the rough edges."

Katie brightened at the aspect of proper decorum. "I'll get 'im 'Chesterfield's Complete Rules of Etiquette.' 'Tis guaranteed ta wear down anything!"

The bell rang upon the shop door, and Mrs. Ida Tarbox entered. The recent widow of a farmer, she was dressed in her usual garments of questionable lineage, and clutched a tired, drab reticule as well as her customary, corncob pipe.

" 'Mornin' all!" she enthused.

Ginnie was always pleased to greet a customer. Even one who wore boots.

"Mrs. Tarbox! How good to see you!"

Ida Tarbox nodded, then fixed a firm gaze upon Cullie.

"De' May Belle's come in. Ya might wanna be at de' levee."

"Miss Ginnie!" exclaimed Katie, "Captain Ross—-!"

Mrs. Tarbox continued. "De' bluebellies're on board. Looks like trouble."

Cullie punched a fist into the palm of his hand. "Have they taken the Captain?"

"Don' know," replied the farm lady. "Two of 'em boarded, jist as she docked. One was a Lieutenant. De' other was a mean-lookin', snake-eyed cuss."

"Then, I'd bes' be goin'," declared Cullie, as he started for the door.

"An', mind yer manners!" demanded Katie. "Dere's ladies about!"

Determining all logic to be useless, Cullie removed his cap. He then made a sweeping bow, turned upon his heel, and departed for the levee. Mrs. Tarbox stood transfixed.

"Didn' know ya could train 'em, like thet."

"Oh, it is indeed, possible," insisted Ginnie. "Though instruction may take several years."

"Huh," mused Ida Tarbox. "Don' have de' time. Besides...what ah really come fer is a bonnet! A gal's gotta have somethin' nice once in 'er life. Mebbe one o' them French things, like in Godey's Fashion Book!"

Ginnie smiled, with an enterprising, enthusiasm. "Katie, the French straw in the window, please!"

A straw bonnet was retrieved. It was adorned with silk ribbons and pink roses, and very much impressed Mrs. Tarbox.

"Busted buckets!" she exulted. "How much fer all this 'frou-frou'?"

"Only five dollars an' fifty cents!" smiled Katie.

" 'Little high-priced fer somethin' ya jis' plop on yer head," elucidated Ida Tarbox.

"It may seem a bit expensive," replied Ginnie, "but one pays for quality. And a French design!"

The farm lady withdrew a knotted handkerchief from the old reticule, and counted out the amount for the be-ribboned article. After thirty years working the farm, Mrs. Tarbox was determined to become as fashionable as possible. And the French bonnet was to be only the beginning.

The lady departed, and the coins were discreetly, locked away. It was then the young milliner divulged a bit of distressing information.

"Have ya heard about Miss Oralee Gibbs?"

Ginnie clipped the twine from her package. "This ribbon is for Miss Oralee's wedding gown. Whyever do you ask?"

Katie interlaced her fingers. "Well...Miss Oralee's young man has joined de' army."

Ginnie looked up from the package. "Then, he has gone South?"

The milliner stared out the display window. Several Federal soldiers passed by, guns poised with bleak authority upon their shoulders. "No, Miss Ginnie. 'E 's gone fer de' Union."

Ginnie was speechless. Oralee Gibbs' family were Secessionists. Her brothers had gone South, months before. There would be no marriage to a man enlisted in the Federal army.

"Oh, Miss Ginnie," exclaimed Katie, "dis war has even divided loved ones! Where it will end?" Having no answer, the young dressmaker could only embrace her milliner, in heartfelt empathy.

The bell upon the shop door rang, and a tall, dark-haired gentleman, dressed in the latest of haberdashery entered, with Cullie at his side.

Ginnie could only smile with delight...but as always, Katie had something to say.

"Why, 'tis 'imself—- Captain Ross!"

Indeed. The man was Owen Ross, captain of the steamer May Belle, the swiftest boat upon the river. Ginnie rushed to greet the one person she had known all her life. Cullie, however, issued an unexpected, warning.

"Careful now," he advised. "De' man's jis' taken de' Oath of Allegiance."

Those words frosted the room with an icy silence. Moments passed, before anyone dared speak. And when someone did...it was Captain Owen Ross.

"As you all know, my allegiance is to the South. I took the Union's 'loyalty oath.' But I made that pledge because I could do more outside the walls of Gratiot Street Prison, than within them."

Ginnie searched the face of her lifelong friend. "The authorities would have imprisoned you?"

"In less than a heartbeat. They know the May Belle has ties with southern ports. And so they have confiscated my livelihood. Perhaps, forever."

"But, why would de' Union need a steamer?" Katie persisted.

Her brother's eyes became alight with anger. "B'cause they need a fast boat. Fer haulin' bluebellies."

Ginnie pondered those words. The May Belle was to transport Federal troops. She faced Owen squarely, and steeled herself for his answer. "And what shall you do now?" she asked.

Owen Ross gave a cryptic smile. "The authorities despise mail-runners. So, I shall become one."

Ginnie looked away. Owen was to carry missives between families in the city, and their men in the Southern army. The punishment for mail-running, was death.

It was Katie who stepped forward, with a quiet resolve. "Captain Ross...dere's ladies who would gladly gather and deliver those letters dat ya bring."

Cullie looked at his sister. For the fir st time, he felt her worth far more than he had ever imagined.

Owen took the young milliner's hand in his. "Thank you, Katie. I knew I could rely upon you and Cullie." Then he turned toward Ginnie, and his eyes flickered with apprehension. Would she collaborate, or would her Northern sentiments overcome their friendship? So much was dependent upon this young dressmaker, whose family was replete with Union pride.

Though under his hopeful gaze, Ginnie grew more constant in her own belief. "I cannot play a part in this, Owen. You know I cannot."

Owen paused. "Your mother was from Boston," he said, "but your father came from Virginia. He was the finest gambler on the Mississippi. He found me a place as a cabin boy. I have been on the river ever since. Until now."

Ginnie's eyes brimmed with tears. There was no denying every word was true. And when she embraced Owen Ross once more, Ginnie Allen knew her fate was inextricably, linked to his.

Suddenly, the bell rang frantically upon the shop door, and a young man stumbled into the room. He was disheveled and wild-eyed. With some surprise, Owen called out his name.

"Tom Donovan—-!"

The young man drew himself to his full height. "I have thought it over, Captain Ross," announced Tom, between breaths. "I shall be going South with you and Cullie."

"Tommy Donovan!" admonished Katie. "Have ya told yer parents an' sisters? Yer de' only son—-!

"Don't be telling me what to do, Katie McCafferty," Tom beseeched. "My family's for the Union. Not me. I can see what that Yankee agent does. Gideon Pike, they call him! Gideon Pike. He's the one who took the May Belle. He and a Lieutenant. I'm going South to fight every Yankee who crosses my path!" Tom Donovan turned to face Owen Ross. "I shall be coming along with you then, Captain...if it's all right."

Owen cast a furtive glance toward Ginnie. Her eyes glistened, but her expression held an intensity that had not been there before. Then with a confident smile, he placed a hand upon the young man's shoulder. "It's all right with me, Tom. It's all right with me."

Ginnie Allen locked the door to her shop that evening, with much trepidation. Never before had she made a decision so quickly, and with so vast a difference from her own beliefs. As she stepped to the sidewalk, her eye caught the figure of a bearded man, standing just across the milling street. The dressmaker felt a sudden shiver, and quickly blended into the bustling crowd. The man scraped a match upon the side of a building. As he lit a cigar, a one-sided smile unfurled upon his lips, and his dark eyes glimmered with a cruel arrogance. The shop on Verandah Row was indeed, a place of interest. And Gideon Pike was never wrong.

Chapter Two ~ The Madam Enters

Lady with Feather Hat

M rs. Brumley was arrayed in a gown of silk taffeta, the rose be-daubed bonnet, and arge Union cockade. There was no doubt as to the ladies' allegiance, as she placed an order for another bonnet. And when Mrs. Tarbox appeared, the rustle of costly fabric swiftly accompanied Mrs. Brumley, out the door.

"Dabnacious Yankees!" complained Ida Tarbox. "Jis' took over de' whole town. Hardly worth a-dressin' up, any more! An' them Germans is a whole army jis' by their selfs!"

The town's large German population did indeed, seem to have dissolved into the ranks of the Union army. One could not walk a street in the city, without Federal soldiers speaking a German dialect. St. Louis had become almost a foreign country, as well as an armed Union camp.

The dressmaker took a folded skirt from a shelf. "Well, despite everything, I am so grateful you have arrived!"

"Wouldn' miss this fer anythin'! Reckon Captain Ross'll be back soon?"

"We expect his return, any day," said Ginnie, as she smoothed the gingham fabric.

The farm lady rubbed her chin. "Ah've jis' been a-wonderin.' How we gonna deliver those letters, safe-like? Them Yankees're always itchin' ta find somethin.' "

"First of all," replied Ginnie, "this undertaking must be discreet. And we should prepare for anything."

Mrs. Tarbox smiled. "Ah kin be quieter than a hoot-owl chasin' a field mouse! An' ah got ma squirrel gun oiled. Jist in case."

Ginnie did not doubt the lady's proficiency with a firearm. The skirt however, would prove far more valuable.

"Ladies' apparel is all we shall need. And this—-is our mode of delivery!"

Ida Tarbox appeared unconvinced.

"Wal, Miss Ginnie...it's a awful nice skirt—-"

Ginnie turned the item inside-out. "But this is not just a skirt! You see? It has pockets in the hem!"

And there—-sewn around the inside hem—-were pockets. Just the size of letters.

"Busted buckets!" exclaimed Mrs. Tarbox. "Them letters'll go right in them hem-pockets! We'll carry 'em all in our skirts!"

"And none shall be the wiser!" asserted Ginnie, with a satisfied smile.

The farm lady appeared delighted at the prospect, and expressed herself in her usual, succinct way.

"We'll bamboozalate 'em! We'll stupidify 'em! Why, we'll even hornswoggle 'em! Them rattle-brained Yankee roosters, is about to be out-foxed by a flock o' sassy, Southern hens!"

Ginnie was gratified by the approval, and Ida Tarbox departed the shop in high spirits. The farm lady would however, continue to maintain her stock of lead shot and small arms.

Katie soon returned from delivering a bonnet to Fifth Street. She was removing her hat, when four women stepped boldly, into the room. Each was dressed in rather striking apparel, and as three of them gazed about and primped, their matron stood fanning, very slowly.

"Good afternoon," said Ginnie, after a lengthy pause.

The languid motion of the fan ceased, and the lady returned the greeting with a formal introduction.

"Good afternoon, Miss Allen. I am Madam Lottie LaTour. This is Tilly Brown...Octavia Jones...and Antoinette Beaumarchais. You have been recommended by Captain Ross."

Ginnie was immediately, perplexed. A disreputable woman knew her name. And apparently, that of Owen Ross!

"You are speaking of Captain Owen Ross...?"

"Indeed," affirmed the Madam. "Captain of the steamer May Belle, now deplorably, in Union hands." The woman gave the dressmaker an appraising glance. "You shall do splendidly!" she smiled.

"I beg your pardon—-!"

The Madam fanned languorously. "Do not be alarmed, Miss Allen. Captain Ross has made the correct assessment. We must have an attractive young lady for the intrigue."

Ginnie looked at the woman. "Intrigue?" she thought.

Madam LaTour groomed her crimson-feathered fan. "I shall tell you why we have come. We are supplying information to the Confederacy. I have managed a "working" relationship, with our city's Police Chief. He has rendered my place of business on Seventh Street, the official resort of Federal officers. Unknowingly, he has provided a superlative circumstance, for acquiring all manner of clandestine information."

The dressmaker was incredulous. "Then, you spy on Yankees?"

"Spy?!" declared the Madam, "Dear me, no! My girls merely, observe. Much more civilized."

Katie had sought to remain silent, but a question volleyed forth, aimed directly at Madam LaTour.

"And how does dis—-enterprise—-concern Miss Ginnie?"

The Madam's eyes swept over Katie. "Ah...the milliner. Pleased to make your acquaintance. Now, to answer—-we must infiltrate a Union Soiree. The young woman we choose must be someone the officers do not know. Captain Ross believes Miss Allen's power of observation is flawless. Any snippet of information could be of vital importance. It could mean life or death, for thousands of men."

Ginnie was aghast. Thousands of lives might depend upon her!

"Of course, you would need a ballgown," specified the Madam.

Oralee Gibbs' half-made gown stood upon a dress form. Antoinette had taken note of it.

"Zere's a dress in zee corner!" she remarked, with admirable simplicity.

"But—-but it's a wedding gown!" stammered Ginnie.

"Not an obstacle!" smiled Madam LaTour. "Octavia shall modify it in her spare time. Now then...what else?"

"Her hair simply, must be fixed," observed Tilly, as she curled several orange tendrils around a finger.

"And her face could use a bit of color," offered Octavia, patting the berry-red patches upon her cheeks.

"Mes oui, très belle!" opined Antoinette. "If she wear zee corset. And, one zat is French!"

Ginnie was willing to end the association there and then, but the Madam was far advanced in her planning.

"My dear girls, I was contemplating an escort!" she admonished, with a touch of exasperation.

The room became uncannily still, as options were considered. Tilly Brown's notion was by far, the best.

"Mr. Dukenfelter..." she offered.

"Mr. Dukenfelter!" echoed Madam LaTour. "Perfect! Despite the ugly rumors. Now, Miss Allen—-there are two things to remember: never display a speck of intelligence. It discourages the men. You must be but a visual delight...the sparkling ornament upon the arm of a gentleman!"

"Then, I need only be decorative?" ventured Ginnie.

"Decorative?"retorted the Madam, "On the contrary! It has been thoroughly proven, that the beauty of a woman is in direct proportion to the loss of cognitive ability, in the vast majority of men! You must act upon this fortunate facticity Miss Allen, and put it to the best of use!"

This was a predicament. Ginnie had never attended a soiree. Now she was to participate, and must be deceitful as well as treasonous. All under the guidance of a scarlet woman. Who was acquainted with Owen Ross.

Madam LaTour meanwhile, directed her small brigade with the mettle of a Southern general. Her "troops" soon had the wedding gown in hand, and all prepared to take their leave. With obliging forethought, Katie had propped open the front door.

"Do not worry, Miss Allen," smiled the Madam. "Everything shall be perfectly, accomplished!"

The young dressmaker crossed her arms. "Indeed," she said. And it was then, the milliner reckoned a certain captain had best be armed with answers, when next he navigated Verandah Row.

Chapter Three ~ Pike's Plan

Man with Beard in Evening Attire

Less than a week had passed, when Gideon Pike paid a visit to the Provost Marshal. Seated upon a comfortable chair, Pike's dark, sinister eyes glanced about the well-appointed room. They missed nothing. A humidor, filled with fine cigars, rested upon a polished desk, and the Federal agent awaited the question which one gentlemen always inquires of another.

"Cigar, Mr. Pike?" queried the Provost Marshal.

"Thank you, Sir," said Pike.

"And all is well in Chicago," observed the Union official. "I have heard there is a special prison for rebels."

Pike smoothly, clipped the end of his cigar. "Ah, yes...Camp Douglas. Fine facility. Eighty acres o' pure hell."

"Admirable! Illinois has all aspects under control. It is not so, in Missouri. The state is a complete uproar. And what of our difficulty in St. Louis?"

Pike leaned back in the chair, and a wicked smile danced upon his lips. "Trust me, Provost Marshal. I'll whip every rebel in the city."

The Federal official smiled. "You seem very determined."

"I am," admitted Pike, as he struck a match.

"Splendid! And I hope you haven't forgotten the Soiree..."

Pike took a puff of imported tobacco. "De' Union Soiree? Wouldn't miss it. An' neither will de' spies."

"Spies?" declared the Provost Marshal. "Why, we have most of them locked in Gratiot Street prison."

Gideon Pike enjoyed another puff of costly tobacco. "Female spies, Provost Marshal. De' worst kind."

The Union official cocked an eyebrow. He had been apprised of Gideon Pike. No man was more efficient—-or lethal—-when investigating clandestine operations. With the sound of a knock, the two men looked toward the office door.

"Come," said the Federal official, with the ring of autocratic authority in his voice.

Lt. Charles Whittaker entered the room. His handsome features were resolute as he saluted the seated men.

The Provost Marshal smiled in recognition. "Ah! Lt. Whittaker! You, of course, know Mr. Pike—-"

"I do, Sir," said Charles, as he made a slight, courteous bow.

Pike nodded, and motioned toward the soldier with his cigar. "Lt. Whittaker is most efficient. Seized de' May Belle with me, a few weeks ago."

The Union official gave a nod. "You appear to be a capable man, Lieutenant. Wounded at Missionary Ridge…"

"Fully recovered, Sir. Soon to rejoin my regiment."

"Ah! Under Grant or Sherman?"

"General Sherman, Sir. With Colonel McCook, and the 52nd Ohio Infantry."

The Provost Marshal leaned forward. "Are you married, Lieutenant?" he asked.

Charles lowered his eyes. "I am afraid I have not had the privilege, Sir."

"De' Lieutenant is a romantic," sneered Pike, as his impassible, dark eyes followed a plume of smoke. "He prob'ly dreams o' de' perfect female. One he would do anything for, no doubt."

The Federal official looked at Pike, then back at Charles. "Mr. Pike has a unique perspective on the ladies. However, your being unencumbered, shall prove most useful!"

Gideon Pike watched another curl of smoke spiral its way to the ceiling.

"Lieutenant," continued the Union official, "there is a young man in town from Boston. He is stopping at the Planter's House Hotel with a relative. His name is William MacGregor, and his father left a sizable bequest to the Federal government. Twenty thousand dollars—-in gold coin."

"A generous gift, Sir," said Charles, grateful for the benevolence to the Northern cause.

"Indeed. Mr. MacGregor and Miss Margaret, his cousin, shall be attending the Union Soiree, as my guests. I should like you to meet them there, as an envoy of the army. And if you might be attentive as well, to the lady…"

"It shall be my honor, Sir," said Charles.

The Federal official leaned back in his chair. "Excellent! I shall arrange an introduction! The event has been placed at a lager haus. Perhaps you know of it. Freudig's Garden."

"I do, Sir," replied Charles. "A surpassing establishment."

"It is, indeed. The Germans have enabled us to retain control of the city, and their celebrations are also, quite admirable. I have heard there is not a better beer garden in St. Louis!"

"Just think of it, Lieutenant," mused Pike. "A whole evening flanking German beer kegs!"

"You just attend your duties, Lieutenant Whittaker," ordered the Provost Marshal. "Mr. Pike has his own priorities."

"Sir!" said Charles, with an impeccable salute.

The Union official smiled. "The Federal army always exceeds itself. That is all, Lieutenant."

Charles turned, and with a decisive stride, left the room. The Provost Marshal leaned forward, and gave Pike an inquisitive look.

"So! You and Lt. Whittaker captured the May Belle—-"

Pike took another puff of the expensive cigar, and squinted through the haze. "It is but a trifle, Sir."

"Trifle? She is quite the prize! The swiftest boat upon the Mississippi river!"

"Can't be beat for speed," admitted Pike, with a crooked smile.

The Federal official leaned back in his chair. "It is regrettable however, that her captain is out of reach."

Gideon Pike's dark, merciless, eyes glinted, as he gazed at the man behind the well-polished, desk. "Only a short reprieve, Provost Marshal. Captain Owen Ross will return. An' when he does...I've a noose with his name on it."

Chapter Four ~ An Unwelcome Surprise

Brown leghorn straw hat with full brown feather and black velvet ribbon

---

Fourth Street was a whirl of dust when Ginnie and Katie arrived at the shop, bearing purchases from Dawson's Drygoods. As they entered, Ginnie was listening to information which, as usual, had been acquired by her milliner.

"Are you quite certain?" asked Ginnie, placing the purchases upon a shelf.

Katie nodded. "De' authorities took ev'ry piece o' Mrs. Parmalee's fine, rosewood furniture. They piled it up in a wagon, then hauled it away ta be sold at auction."

Ginnie shuddered as she removed her bonnet. Without a piece of evidence, Mrs. Parmalee had been assessed hundreds of dollars for being a Secessionist. When the lady had no money to pay the fine, the authorities confiscated her furniture. And now there was talk that women would be be arrested for any seeming loyalty to the South. Ginnie began to feel an intense anger toward Federal domination within the city.

"We shall do whatever we can, for Mrs. Parmalee," she vowed. "And if I ever associate with another Yankee—-it shall be far too soon!"

The bell upon the shop door rang, and a young lady and gentleman entered. As he removed his hat, the gentleman chanced upon Katie.

"Good morning, Miss...Allen?"

"Beggin' yer pardon, sir..." said Katie, and quickly motioned to the proprietress.

Ginnie hesitated. These two people were not from St. Louis. "Good morning!" she offered, feigning cheerfulness. "May I be of assistance?"

The pretty but sullen, young woman did not seem enthusiastic about the visit. Her face was framed by an expensive bonnet, and she studied the shop with a regal indifference.

"Miss Allen!" smiled the young man, "I am William MacGregor! My cousin...Miss Margaret MacGregor."

Miss MacGregor did not exhibit a smile. In fact, the only movement she performed was to arch an an eyebrow in unconcealed contempt.

"A pleasure to make your acquaintance," replied Ginnie. "May I present Miss Katherine McCafferty, my milliner."

Katie's face dimpled, and William was charmed. Margaret was far less pleased.

"Really, William. Whyever, are we here?" she demanded.

"Well, Cousin—-" William began.

"I should never make a purchase from a shop like this!" announced Margaret.

"I beg your pardon!" declared Ginnie.

Margaret tilted an aristocratic chin. "Your room is dingy, and déclassé, Miss Allen. Needless to say."

Ginnie stared in disbelief. This was a new form of etiquette, indeed.

"And there is not a French modiste, on the premises!" sniffed Margaret. "Hardly as genteel as shops in Boston!"

Katie inched toward the wall, but William crossed his arms, and smiled. Ginnie curled her fingers around a very sharp scissor, then turned to face her adversary.

"Miss MacGregor! Although this is not the room of a society couturier, I assure you, we have a superior knowledge of the prevailing, French fashion. And that would embrace whatever microscopic information you might care to provide!" Ginnie gave a defiant nod, then cut the twine upon her package.

"How dare you!" exclaimed Margaret. "William—-!"

William stood with his arms still crossed, in apparent enjoyment of the controversy. "Quite remarkable," he reflected. "Like peas-in-a-pod!"

Margaret observed the change in her cousin. "Peas in a—-have you lost your senses, Will MacGregor?!"

"On the contrary," clarified William, "I am unabashedly, rational."

Margaret hesitated, then pointed directly toward the source of her dismay. Ginnie squared her shoulders, and stared back, with all the might she could muster.

"But she has insulted me!" emphasized Margaret.

"Yes. And quite handsomely!" smiled William.

Miss MacGregor stood, speechless. Why would her cousin not defend her?

"Do compose yourself," pleaded William. "There is a purpose to this, I promise!"

Margaret turned upon her cousin, with a flash of anger. "Purpose? If I am here to buy, I shall refuse to purchase a single, wooden button from that—-that seamstress!"

Ginnie cast a gaze of undisguised hatred upon Margaret, and their eyes locked in unspoken hostility.

"Now, ladies," beseeched William, "Do try to be calm!"

"Mr. MacGregor," implored Ginnie, "please state your intention, as to this meeting."

"Indeed!" demanded Margaret. "And be done with it, quickly!"

William nodded. "And, so I shall. Miss Allen…after your father passed on, your mother traveled back to the family home, in Boston. You were left here, in the care of your grandmother. That was eighteen years ago. In Boston, your mother was hastily married to my uncle. But she had carried a secret with her…all the way from St. Louis."

Ginnie was instantly, curious. "A secret—-?"

William nodded. "Entrusted to my father. To be disclosed only upon his passing."

"Humph!" smirked Margaret. "A secret about her mother. Thank goodness, it has nothing to do with me!"

"Ah, but Margaret," replied William, "it has everything to do with you. You see—-YOU—-were the secret!"

A chilling wave of reality, swept over the two young women. Only William MacGregor seemed to be gratified by the long-delayed disclosure.

"And, there it is," he rhapsodized, "revealed, at last! The two of you are utterly, legally, and undeniably—-"

"Sisters—-?!" decried Ginnie, and Margaret, in unison. Neither could believe this terrible twist of Destiny, and unfortunate Fate. Sisters. This was a most unwelcome surprise!

"I think that went rather, well!" admitted William to Katie, who was beginning to believe he was the nicest young man she had ever known. "Now then, Miss Allen—-Cousin Ginnie—-" said William, "there is to be a Union Soiree on Saturday, next. Please honor us by joining our company!"

Ginnie quickly seized upon the idea. "Why, Cousin—-I should be delighted!"

Margaret however, appeared intent upon keeping the familial relationship to an absolute minimum.

"I do hope this sordid discovery is kept quiet as possible!" she asserted, as she tightened the ribbons upon her extravagant bonnet.

"Oh, indeed, sister," agreed Ginnie. "I refuse to breathe a single word!"

Margaret seemed assured. "Then I hope there shall be no further, awkward, surprises."

Those words were barely accomplished, when the bell rang upon the shop door. Four women stepped boldly, into the room. Each was dressed in rather striking apparel...and they carried what looked exactly like the bodice and skirt of a ballgown. Margaret stared at the vision in absolute horror, then at her new-found sister. At that moment, Ginnie reckoned there was only one thing to do. She looked directly at Margaret. And smiled.

Chapter Five ~ The Grandest Game

Planters House Hotel on Fourth Street

The Planter's House was known as the finest hotel west of the Mississippi, and was frequented only by those who could afford the luxury. "Planter's Punch," was served by a bartender whose diamond rings and cufflinks twinkled with his every move. Residing in this rarefied atmosphere, William and Margaret MacGregor enjoyed the finer life. And Katie McCafferty was content to pass the edifice each morning, upon her way to earn a living. This day however, was to be very different.

William took a step from the crowded hotel vestibule, and spied Katie, making her way down Fourth Street. "Miss McCafferty!" he called out, despite the social impropriety of doing so.

At the sound of her name Katie turned, causing the ribbons upon her hat to flutter. "Mr. MacGregor!" she exclaimed, astonished by the young man's boldness.

William wound his way through the multitude of guests to meet her. "I have often, seen you pass by," he said, with a tip of his hat.

" 'Tis de' shortest way ta Verandah Row," answered Katie, with a blush.

William gave an affectionate smile. "May I walk with you? I have something of importance to ask."

Katie nodded, and he stepped beside her. She wore a new straw hat, with silk ribbons that trailed down her back. William noticed the ribbons matched her eyes to perfection.

"Miss McCafferty," he began, "the question I have is upon a subject of my particular interest. I am about to pursue an endeavor, and must know if you consider the effort worthwhile."

They had come to the end of the street. Katie looked up at William, who appeared very serious, indeed.

"Whatever is it, Mr. MacGregor?"

William looked down onto Katie's luminous, upturned face. He took a deep breath.

"Miss McCafferty...do you know anything about—-about the game of Base Ball?"

There was a bit of a pause.

"Well, Mr. MacGregor...me brother plays de' game."

William was overjoyed. "Excellent fellow! Is he here, in the city?"

Katie paused. "Well... 'e's out o' town at de' moment. But Cullie McCafferty is a hurler—-an' good one!"

William clasped his gloved hands, together. Here was a man who could pitch! And a hurler was exactly what he needed! "Miss McCafferty—-I am about to fit up a Base Ball team!"

Katie's eyes widened. "Holy angels!" she declared. Cullie had always wished to join a Base Ball team.

"I must know if you think the notion worthwhile—-" William beseeched, seeking agreement from the young woman he adored.

Katie's ribbons played softly, with the morning breeze. "Shall dere be caps an' uniforms?"

"The best that money can buy," decreed William, "with fine stitchery upon the shirt fronts!"

"An' ya'll pay 'de' men well, fer playin' de' game?"

"Indeed, I shall! And, most particularly...the man who pitches!"

Katie could scarcely, contain her excitement. "Oh, Mr. MacGregor! 'Twill be a wondrous endeavor! But why did ya need my thoughts, upon it?"

William looked into the eyes that so perfectly matched fluttering ribbons, in the breeze. "Because one day, Miss McCafferty, Base Ball shall be known as the grandest game in the world. And I should like you there to see it...with me."

Then William MacGregor offered his arm, and though he was a Unionist, the young milliner linked her arm through his. Someday, she would tell him all about Cullie. But today was not that day.

Chapter Six ~ Meeting the Enemy

Two Women wearing Day Look

Though the Union Soiree was that evening, Ginnie was determined to visit Dawson's Drygoods. The last patron had departed, and she was tying on her bonnet, when her sister entered the room. Without a word, Margaret raised the veil upon her hat, and looked about.

"If you are seeking my milliner, she is purchasing trim."

"Whyever do you employ her?" queried Margaret. "She is a rebel, if I ever saw one. And if I had evidence, I would go straight to the authorities!"

"Oh, Margaret..." sighed Ginnie, as she straightened her collar.

"And you always, defend her!" complained Margaret. "I could almost believe you are a Secessionist! And William is infatuated with her! Men. I shall never marry. There is not a man good enough in the entire Union! And where shall you be going? The Soiree is but, hours away!"

Ginnie took up a velvet reticule. "Dawson's has organdy. I shan't be long."

"And, what am I to do?" asked Margaret, with a petulance inspired by years of good breeding.

"Well, you might tend to the shop," offered Ginnie, on her way to the door.

I'll not lift a finger for anyone!"

"How very agreeable, sister. I am sure everyone shall be delighted!"

The front door closed, and Margaret began to pout. She continued in this manner, until there was a knock upon the back door. Uncertain of the consequences, she dropped her veil, then opened the latch. A man rushed in, glanced about the room, then placed a valise beneath a poplin gown, suspended from a dress form. He turned, and for an instant, Margaret's eyes met his. Then a clamorous voice from the street assaulted their ears.

"In here, Magee!" ordered Gideon Pike.

The unknown man seated himself upon a chair by the display window. He shook open a morning newspaper, which he proceeded to read, with great interest. Margaret turned, just as Gideon Pike and Officer Michael Magee entered the room. Their leather shoes pounded a heavy tattoo upon the painted floor, and the Federal agent stopped short, upon seeing the lady. In vain, he attempted to comprehend the face behind the translucent, gauze veiling.

"Good afternoon, Miss...Gideon Pike. I work for the Provost Marshal. Have you seen a man come by, just now?"

"A gentleman, Mr. Pike?"

"Hardly a gentleman, Miss," corrected Pike.

"Perhaps he absconded to an establishment?" proposed Margaret.

"Dere's a tavern at de' corner," observed Officer Magee.. "De' scoundrel might be dere—-"

Gideon Pike pondered the notion. Occasionally, the City Police produced a competent idea.

"Then search de' tavern, Magee," he commanded. "An' don't lay a finger on de' liquor."

Officer Magee, mindful of regulations, departed to pursue his duty. Then Pike's dark eyes roved about the room. They settled upon the man with the early edition newspaper.

"Who's that?" Pike demanded, as he stabbed a finger in the unknown man's direction.

Margaret hardly, hesitated. "That? Why...that is the porter. His deliveries are quite expeditious!"

"The porter, huh? Thank you, Miss. I'll remember that."

Margaret nodded, and Gideon Pike set out to supervise Officer Magee. For a moment, all was still. Then with a rustle, the newspaper dropped, and the unknown man peered through the display window. As he did, Margaret silently, appraised him. Then the visitor faced his benefactress.

"Thank you," he said, with wholehearted, sincerity.

Margaret was intrigued. "And whom do I have the pleasure of defending?"

"Owen Ross," the stranger replied. "Captain Owen Ross."

"Captain—?" queried Margaret.

Owen shook his head. "That is of no consequence. However, you were very daring, Missus—-?"

Margaret raised her veil. "Miss," she emphasized. "Miss Margaret MacGregor."

Owen studied the delicate face before him. Beauty and bravery did not always mix. And though he wondered who Margaret MacGregor was, the Confederate letters in the valise were of utmost importance.

"Then Miss...if you would tell Ginnie—-Miss Allen—-that I've delivered the article...I'd be much obliged."

"I shall do that, Captain."

"Then, I thank you, again. Good day...Miss MacGregor."

Margaret stared at the back door for quite some time, even after her sister returned from Dawson's. And Ginnie sensed a difference in Margaret, almost immediately.

"Are you ill, sister?" she asked.

"I am perfectly well!" asserted Margaret. "A Captain Ross has left an item, under the poplin. I daresay, he appeared acquainted with you. Is he your beau?"

"Certainly not!"

"Well, I suppose there is a wife..." replied Margaret.

"Wife? On the contrary—" declared the dressmaker.

Margaret stood in quiet contemplation, and Ginnie gazed at her, intently. Something had happened, but what? And now there was a valise which needed concealment, on the very night of the Soiree! Owen could not have chosen a worse time to return.

The bell upon the shop door rang, and Katie stepped into the room with a hatbox.

" 'Afternoon, Miss Ginnie," she smiled, until she saw Margaret.

Margaret arched an eyebrow, then concentrated her attention upon Ginnie.

"Do be on time this evening. I shall not be made late for the Soiree!"

"Indeed, sister," sighed Ginnie.

"Oh, yes—-" added Margaret, "an escort has been arranged for you. A Lieutenant, I believe."

"A Lieutenant—-?"

"It was the best we could do. Grant was preoccupied, and Sherman was busy."

"How very thoughtful," said Ginnie, thankful a Mr. Duckenfelter would not be necessary.

Margaret smoothed a sleeve. "Just do not be tardy. I must maintain some social standing, in St. Louis!"

Ginnie nodded, and Margaret departed. Then Katie crossed her arms and made a concise observation.

"If yer sister was a gun…she'd be a two-ton howitzer."

"Never mind that!" declared Ginnie. "Owen has delivered the letters!"

Katie was scandalized when the valise was retrieved, yet agreed under the poplin gown was as good a hiding place, as any. The missives however, were in need of a much better refuge.

"I shall take the valise to Mrs. Campbell," asserted Ginnie. "We shall hide it among her her husband's leather goods."

The choice being made, Katie bent to latch the valise. A scrawl of familiar handwriting caught her eye.

" 'Tis a letter from Cullie!" she exclaimed, and took hold of the unexpected correspondence.

Ginnie smiled and covered the valise with a large, paisley shawl. She was grateful the Campbells had kept their Southern sympathies well-hidden, and their leather goods emporium was only a short distance from her door.

"I shan't be long," she said…then stepped onto Fourth Street.

Katie quickly opened the worn, folded paper. There before her was laid bare the tribulations of war. And as tears ran in small, rivulets down her cheeks, she longed to see her only brother, just once more. Then the precious letter was folded, and placed safely, within her apron pocket.

The paisley shawl was empty when the dressmaker returned. Her thoughts drifted to her father, and his expertise at playing cards. She knew, however, the game she was about to enter would be far different. Ginnie Allen was about to gamble with her life.

The shawl was folded, and placed upon a shelf. "The letters are well-hidden," she said. Then her trembling hand found itself to her throat. Could she truly do all that was needed?

"Oh Miss Ginnie," begged Katie, "ya mus' be brave! An' look! Here's somethin' jist fer dis eve'nin'!"

Katie opened the hatbox, and reached within its the depths. Slowly, she withdrew a shimmering headdress. It sparkled in the declining sunlight like a wreath of diamonds. "Oh," Ginnie breathed, "it's exquisite!"

"Dere's not another like it. 'Tis jist a bit of ammunition!"

Ginnie wavered at the words. "Ammunition?"she asked.

"Indeed! When a lady dresses, 'tis like girding fer battle. She needs all de' proper weaponry!"

Why, of course! A Soiree was merely a fashion battlefield. Each lady would be sumptuously dressed—-in her very best munitions—-vying for total victory! And while the Union officers were beguiled by the extravagance...the gathering of clandestine information would be practically effortless! Ginnie's confidence soared, along with newfound appreciation for every probable armament she possessed. Within moments, she hailed her milliner.

"Katherine McCafferty...it is high time, I dressed. And tonight—-we shall bring use heavy artillery!"

Chapter Seven ~ Freudig's Garden

Cadet Hop

The Union Soiree had begun. It was a brilliant affair, with ladies in jewel-hued gowns, and officers in blue dress uniforms. The merry clink of beer steins, and the delicate tinkling of wineglasses intermingled with every conversation and joyous burst of laughter. Freudig's Garden was alive with delicious food, drink, music...and romance.

As the orchestra struck up a waltz, Margaret and William entered the glimmering hall, and Lt. Charles Whittaker crossed the floor to meet them.

"Good evening, Miss MacGregor...Mr. MacGregor!" he smiled.

"Lt. Whittaker!" replied William, as he shook hands with the Lieutenant. "A pleasure, to see you!"

"The pleasure is mine, sir," said Charles, who then turned toward Margaret with a small, gracious bow.

"How kind you are, Lieutenant." smiled Margaret. "We anticipate my sister Miss Allen, momentarily. I am afraid she mislaid a glove."

William grinned. "As you know Lieutenant...the ladies cannot do without their accessories!"

"Indeed, not!" agreed Charles. "If acceptable, I shall wait here, for Miss Allen. The Provost Marshal is very much anticipating your presence."

"Excellent, Lieutenant...thank you! Shall we, Margaret?"

Margaret placed a be-gloved hand upon William's arm, and the two crossed the candle-lit floor. But a moment later Ginnie entered the room, the erstwhile wedding dress now transformed into a diaphanous ball-gown. She appeared to shimmer in the candlelight, and a trio of 2nd Lieutenants abandoned decorum, and rushed to greet her.

"Good evening, Miss!" declared the first.

"'Evening, ma'am!" exclaimed the second.

"Guten Abend, Fraulein!" proclaimed the third.

The sudden attention left Ginnie flustered, and it was Charles who stepped up to the small assemblage.

"Miss Allen? I am Lt. Charles Whittaker, your escort for the festivities." He nodded at the hopeful suitors. "May you have a pleasant evening, gentlemen." The young men made their bows, then scattered into the jubilant gathering.

Charles faced the lady he had championed. "I apologize for the presumption. Fortunately, I rank them."

"Oh, thank goodness, for that!" answered Ginnie, striving to appear as vacuous as possible. "I do apologize for being late, Lieutenant. It was foolish of me to drop my glove—-"

With a reassuring voice, Charles replied, "A delay is but Fate creating Destiny, Miss Allen."

Ginnie thrilled at the words, and found it difficult to continue her deception. "How poetic you are, sir!" she said.

"My mother was once a schoolteacher," admitted Charles. "It was her favorite adage."

"And yet, you have become a soldier..."

"My father graduated West Point, and wished I do the same. The army has certainly not lacked in providing places of interest."

The young dressmaker paused. "Then, may a beer garden be a place of such curiosity?"

Charles was delighted at the charming conversation. "Indeed! Especially if the beer garden were in a French town, on the Mississippi River."

With pleasant surprise, their laughter intermingled. Then Ginnie remembered the true reason she stood by the officer's side.

"Your...duties in St. Louis must be consequential, sir."

Charles' smile disappeared. "I am here awaiting transfer, but seem to have become more useful to Mr. Pike."

Ginnie, at once recollected the name, but needed further insight. "Mr. Pike?" she queried.

"A Federal agent. We have requisitioned several steamboats for the Union."

Ginnie suppressed a shudder. This was the Lieutenant, Tom Donovan had mentioned. She looked into the face of the man before her, whose quiet demeanor spoke so well of him. A man whom she could very easily, love. Then with a sudden jolt, a loud voice emanated from the crowded floor, and Gideon Pike shouted over the lively pace of a polka.

"Ah—-Lieutenant Whittaker!"

Charles turned toward the man with the pitiless, dark eyes. "Mr. Pike—-" he said, with no desire to pursue the acquaintance, for the evening. The Federal agent however, was upon a mission of his own.

" 'Appears to be quite de' gala!" observed Gideon Pike, as he withdrew a cigar from his coat. "Nobody can outdo the Germans, at a beer festival." Spitefulness lurked behind his one-sided smile, and he motioned toward Ginnie, with the cigar. He knew female spies could be anywhere, and if startled—-like birds—-they would take flight. He just had to flush them out. "Won't you make an introduction, Lieutenant?"

Charles hesitated, but accepted the social obligation. "Miss Allen...permit me to present you to Mr. Pike."

Ginnie made a small curtsy, as Pike's barbarous eyes scanned her face and gown. Then he squinted, as was his custom, while attempting to remember some important detail.

"Allen..." he mused. "Don't you keep a storefront on Verandah Row?"

"It—-it is but a small shop for ladies—-" stammered Ginnie, surprised by the inquiry.

There was a breathless moment, then Pike snapped his fingers. "One, thirty-two—-de' place with de' porter!"

Ginnie managed a faint smile. Mr. Pike had obtained far more information than he should have.

"Is all this necessary, Sir?" demanded Charles, with a frown.

"Lieutenant," said Pike, "I'm from Chicago. Things are done differently, there. Tonight however, seems a time for jollification. So be it! Enjoy de' celebration, sir. And, you...Miss Allen."

With the cigar clenched firmly between his teeth, Pike swerved and shouldered his way back into the crowd.

Charles leaned toward Ginnie. "I am sorry, Miss Allen. Mr. Pike rarely separates work from pleasure."

Ginnie trembled. "He seems a man of uncommon tenacity."

"His expertise is greatly appreciated by the Union," admitted Charles. "He does what he says he will do."

Ginnie's next words came quickly. Far too quickly. "Then, Mr. Pike is a spy for the North—-?"

Charles lingered upon the question. Could this young woman have ties to the South? He proceeded with caution, and on the chance his suspicion was correct, offered a warning. "Not as such," he answered. "Mr. Pike has many duties. He believes women are involved in clandestine activities. And I have found that Mr. Pike will stop at nothing, Miss Allen. Absolutely, nothing."

The rustle of fine silk filled the room, and swirling dancers glimmered softly, in the candlelight. Ginnie and Charles stood together in silence, each in their own attempt to comprehend the enormity of their meeting—-a meeting made far more complicated by the war, loyalty...and Mr. Gideon Pike.

For a moment the music ceased, and with fans aflutter, each dancer mingled with their partner. When the orchestra struck up another waltz, Ginnie understood she must not only complete her undertaking, but appear the least suspicious, as possible.

"The music is beginning, Lieutenant," she observed. "It appears to be a tune by Strauss!"

Charles laughed softly, and offered his hand. "Then may I have this waltz, Miss Allen—-before the orchestra discovers the sheet music to the 'Race Horse Galop?'"

The remainder of the evening was spent enjoying the delights of the Soiree. Gideon Pike kept watch, but could not readily discern if the dressmaker was a Confederate. For her part, Ginnie gleaned information from several conversations—-all the while falling deeply in love with the Lieutenant. And after his first dance with her, Charles Whittaker no longer cared if the young woman he squired was a Unionist, or the enemy. He could only feel in his heart, that he had found the partner Fate had created, and Destiny had ordained.

Chapter Eight ~ Confederate Mail

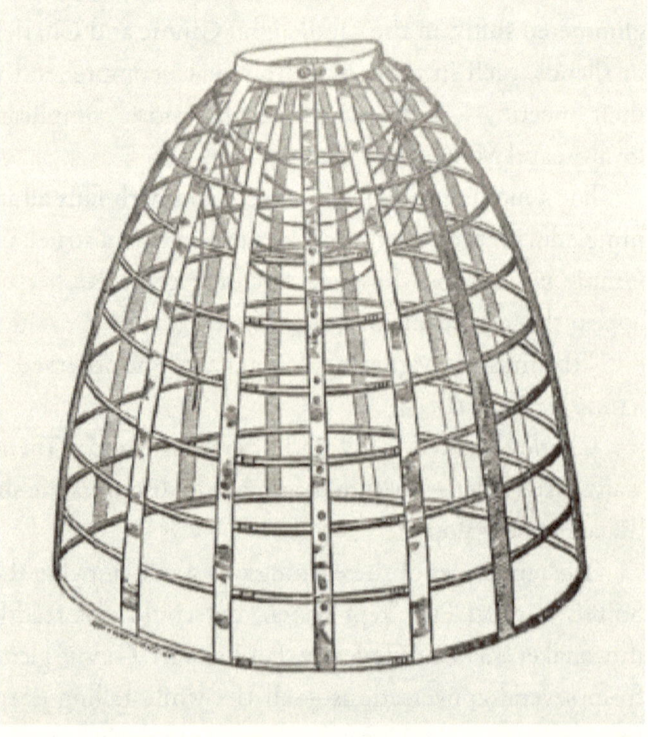

Birdcage Hoop Skirt

As the late-Spring sun rose over the Illinois horizon, Mrs. Tarbox arrived at the shop with letters gathered in her skirt. Ginnie and Katie had also collected missives, and the valise began to burgeon with its priceless contents. The skirts and their hem-pockets had performed admirably. But Gideon Pike sensed collusion, and he awaited the smallest of mistakes.

"Reckon that's it," said Ida Tarbox, as she smoothed her gingham skirt. "Thar's a pile of 'em from Fifth Street."

Katie wiped her brow. "Those ladies had plenny ta write! De' valise is full ta de' very brim!"

"Jis' pack 'em in tight," advised Mrs. Tarbox. "Them letters is, prob'ly, 'bout de' Belle Memphis!"

"Ah, what a hateful thing that was, ta do," replied Katie. "Five ladies...put aboard a steamer, an' banished from de' city. An' their poor, little children left cryin' by themselves, at de' levee!"

The milliner tearfully, placed the valise beneath the millinery table, while the farm lady's anger intensified.

"Thet tin-hearted bluebelly snared 'em, slick as a whistle. They was was burnin' evidence, an' 'e caught 'em red-handed!"

Katie wiped away a tear, and took a deep breath. They, themselves, had been fortunate...so far.

Suddenly, a firm knock was heard upon the front door. Both women started at the sound.

"De' shop is closed!" announced Katie, with a quaver in her voice.

The person outside was insistent, as well as familiar. "It is Madam LaTour. I desperately, must enter!"

Katie unlocked the door, and the Madam brushed past her in a flash of scintillating color.

"Close it, quickly!" she ordered. "I am not usually about at this hour, and it may seem a trifle suspicious. But when I see a hat like the one in your window, I simply must have it before someone else!"

Mrs. Tarbox stood stunned by the lady's vivid ensemble.

"Busted buckets! Thet color could burn fuzz off'n a peach!"

"It is fuchsine," explained the Madam. "A French import."

"From Pair-ee?" inquired Ida Tarbox.

"The very place," smiled Madam LaTour.

"Wal, ah'll be pickled," declared the farm lady.

"Indeed," replied the Madam, as she turned to Katie. "Miss McCafferty—-the black straw in the window, please!"

The hat was a woven black straw, decorated with a scarlet plume and matching silk ribbons. Madam LaTour applied the new head-wear, and quickly took up a looking glass.

"How divine!" she enthused. "I usually forswear black in my wardrobe, but one must have some sort of funereal attire, these days."

Mrs. Tarbox continued to express her admiration.

"Thet outfit shore is a mule-stopper!" she proclaimed.

The Madam smiled, once again. "You are too kind," she said.

Ida Tarbox nodded, then gave a farewell, as Katie opened the door.

"Many thanks fer yer help," said Katie, as a stream of sunlight splashed upon the floor.

"Jis' doin' mah duty," intoned Mrs. Tarbox. "An' you be careful. Thet snake-eyed cuss is ev'rywhar."

With the farm lady's departure, Madam LaTour requisitioned the chair at the millinery table.

"Miss Allen certainly outdid herself at the Union Soiree," she announced, adjusting a ribbon.

"Did she, now?" replied Katie.

The lady from Seventh Street placed the looking glass upon the table. "Indeed. We now, have certain knowledge that General Sherman is massing troops in Chattanooga, Tennessee. And how do you suppose, he shall direct those soldiers?"

"Soldiers? Holy angels! I've never thought of it!"

"Then, think, Miss McCafferty!" demanded the Madam. "If you were a Union General, and had 100,000 men at your disposal, what would you do?"

"Well...would I march them somewhere?" asked Katie in almost a whisper.

"Exactly!" affirmed Madam LaTour, as she stood and removed the hat. "I believe the General shall march his troops straight through the State of Georgia. This is a man who could destroy the Confederacy."

With that fateful prediction, the bell upon the shop door rang. Neither woman was surprised when Gideon Pike tramped heavily, into the room. Cigar smoke trailed in his wake, and not a moment was spent on pleasantries.

"I'm lookin' for Miss Allen," he growled. "She here?"

"Not yet, sir," answered Katie.

The Madam adjusted her bonnet, while Pike's dark, prying, eyes darted about the shop. Confederate evidence could be anywhere. He just had to find it.

"I believe I shall have this hat," smiled Madam LaTour, as she handed the black straw to Katie.

The milliner went to fetch a hatbox, and the Madam languidly, tied her bonnet ribbons. Gideon Pike began to pace. He was not a man familiar with being detained.

Madam LaTour glanced at the Federal agent. "Excuse me, sir! You seem an estimable Union man. Is it possible you've not visited my excellent, establishment on Seventh Street?"

Pike ceased his perambulation, and removed the cigar. His dark eyes filled with resentful rage. "Not only is it not possible, Madam, but it's not plausible, not probable...and highly unlikely, it'll ever happen."

"How very sad," said Madam LaTour. " Then as a business-lady, I shall make no further demand upon your time."

"Business-lady? Now that implies some sort of intelligence. An' I haven't met a female with any reliable comprehension, since I came to this town!"

"Then I fear you have been most unfortunate in your associations, Mr. Pike," condoled the Madam.

Pike's eyes glittered like cold, black glass. "Women lack the intelligence of men. They have no thought, no judgement...why, females like you, think women should have all de' privileges of men—-prob'ly even de' right to vote!

Madam LaTour paused. "As you are well aware, Mr. Pike, women have no voice in the matter." The lady made her purchase and began to exit, but Gideon Pike would not give up the quarrel.

"An' I guarantee women'll "have no voice in de' matter," for a very long time."

"Indeed," replied the Madam. as she made her way to the front door.

Pike sneered. He wished only to expound his hallowed philosophy upon this renegade of a woman. "An' it's a well-known fact that in civilized society, only men should do de' thinking!"

Madam LaTour turned toward her intractable tutor. "Yes," she agreed. "Men should do the thinking. And perhaps someday, they shall even master it. Good day...Mr. Pike."

The Madam departed and Katie edged away from the Federal agent. She knew he considered every Secessionist woman a sworn enemy. His cruel belligerence was always coiled for an unrelenting, strike upon whatever Southern affiliation he might find. All he needed was tangible evidence.

"A female who can 'think,' is a menace ta society," snarled Pike. And then his foot struck something.

Gideon Pike looked down, and Katie's frightened gaze, followed his. Their eyes fell upon Owen's leather valise.

"What's this?" queried Pike, his dark eyes glinting with suspicion.

Katie forced herself to think of something—-anything—-that would not sound incriminatory.

"Oh—-that b'longs to a customer! She was takin' it to 'er husband, an' 'twas left by mistake! I'll jist move it outta de' way—-"

Katie lifted the heavy valise as best she could, but did not realize an envelope had fallen upon the floor. An envelope that Pike saw, and swiftly pocketed.

"So, it was a mistake, you say?" repeated Pike, as he silently rejoiced over this one small, but significant occurrence.

Katie placed the valise far from the Federal agent. "Yes, sir!" she said, with an inward cringe. "A foolish mistake!"

Gideon Pike gave a crooked smile. "Then let us hope de' "lady" is more careful in de' future. I'll take my leave, now. 'Cussed if I wait, any longer!" Heavy footsteps accompanied his departure, but he turned at the front door. "Oh—-an' be sure to tell Miss Allen, that I shall…remain in contact." He clenched the cigar between his teeth, and closed the door behind him.

Verandah Row was just beginning to awaken, as the Federal agent left the shop. The dry, grating tumult of jostling wagons…the pungent smell of horses glistening in the sun…the insistent cries of street vendors—-all accompanied Pike on the way to his lodging. There, he placed the letter upon a table. Here, finally, was the evidence he had sought for so long. Southern sympathizers were simply spies for the Confederacy, and he would rid the city of them, one by one. And if those spies happened to be women…then all the better.

Chapter Nine ~ Unforeseen

Straw Hat with Flowers

The month of May had turned to June, and the air was redolent with summer. The day began filled with sunlight, but regiments of clouds soon marched across the sky. Katie called at another residence on Fifth Street, that morning. There, she delivered not only a richly feathered hat—-but sixteen letters to five anxious ladies attending a sewing circle. By late afternoon, all the women had sewn a skirt. And each contained hem pockets.

That same morning, Ginnie visited Mrs. Parmalee. She carried several letters from the lady's husband, who was in Georgia, with the Army of Tennessee. Each missive was greatly cherished.

As the dressmaker returned to the shop, lightening had begun to rip and dazzle, and as she removed her leghorn bonnet, the bell upon the shop door rang. But it was not a patron who entered the room. It was Charles Whittaker.

"Lt. Whittaker!" smiled Ginnie, as she smoothed her hair.

"Good morning, Miss Allen," said Charles, as he closed an umbrella and removed his hat.

"Please, Lieutenant—-do come in!"

Charles set the umbrella by the door. "I shan't stay long," he replied.

Ginnie gazed at the Lieutenant, with sudden anxiety. "The army has you employed in this weather?"

"I believe weather has rarely, surmounted the U.S. army. I have come to tell you...I must take my leave of St. Louis."

"Take your leave—?"

"Yes. My orders are to board the May Belle."

The young dressmaker looked away. The May Belle. The fastest boat upon the river.

"Then you are to rejoin your regiment," she replied, her voice as hollow as her heart.

Charles nodded. "Within the hour."

Ginnie fell silent...her thoughts dark, with unfathomable despair. He was a Federal soldier. She was a purveyor for the South. What more could be said? But Charles had determined there was much more to express.

"Miss Allen—-Mr. Pike has found a letter here, upon the floor. A Confederate letter. He shall use it as evidence, against you. There is nothing I can do but tell you of his plan."

Ginnie placed a hand to her throat. The inevitable had come to pass. "Thank you, Lieutenant. I realize—-as a Union officer—-you needn't have cautioned, me."

Charles looked at her in earnest. "My dear, Miss Allen—-I would do anything, for you! Have you still, any regard for me? Any regard, at all?"

Ginnie faced him, and her eyes filled with tears. How could she have doubted their love for each other? "Oh, Lieutenant Whittaker...I have the deepest regard for you. And always, will."

With those few words, Charles' fears were forgotten.

"Dearest Ginnie...it cannot be our fault we are on opposing sides of this war. If I could change the world, I would. Now all I can hope is that, after the fighting is finished...I shall come back—-and find you, again."

It was then, the dressmaker embraced the only man she would ever love. And as Charles stepped to the door, she untied a blue, silk ribbon from her hair and placed it within his hands. He would carry the ribbon as long as he lived. Once more they embraced, then Charles disappeared into the now-blustering, storm. As Ginnie wiped away tears, she quavered at at the thought of the merciless, Federal agent. But there was nothing to be done. The bell rang upon the shop door, and Margaret entered the room. She was attired as always, in a fashionable Boston gown. This time punctuated by a rain-drenched umbrella.

"Inclement weather!" she fretted, dabbing raindrops from her skirt. "And Lt. Whittaker was rushing down the street, with but a hat to protect him!"

Ginnie looked toward the door. The forgotten item was resting beside it. "His umbrella—-" she cried.

Her sister was uncommonly, surprised. "The Lieutenant was here?"

Ginnie took up the umbrella. "Yes. He is rejoining his regiment. I must hurry!"

"Do take mine, as well," insisted Margaret. "It shall be needed upon your return!"

Ginnie accepted the offer, and was quickly on her way. Margaret arched an elegant eyebrow. A Federal officer had been calling! Surely that was proof her sister was a Unionist. Then she sighed, and began to inspect her head-wear. Thankfully, the rain had not spoiled her ribbons. There was nothing worse than rain-spotted silk. A knock at the back door however, rearranged her priorities, and Margaret was not surprised to find who was there.

"Captain Ross! You have an overwhelming propensity, for entering the wrong doors."

Owen removed his hat. "I apologize, Miss MacGregor. It is simply, by habit."

Margaret stepped away from the rain-besieged Captain. "And you are completely, soaked through!"

"I am afraid that cannot be helped, as well," Owen shrugged.

With a demure smile, Margaret looked up at Owen. "I would think a Union man would plan his adventures in a less perplexing way!"

The pause that followed was an uncomfortable one. Then Owen broke the lingering silence. "I am not for the Union," he said.

Margaret felt the color fade from her face. This man was a rebel.

"Have—-have you come, for something?" she managed to ask.

"A mens' valise. Might you know where it is?"

"M-Miss McCafferty...p-places items...beneath the millinery table..." stammered Margaret, as she sought to calm herself at the much unwanted, and unforeseen disclosure.

Owen retrieved the hand luggage. "I am obliged as always, Miss MacGregor."

"And I shall be obliged, to never see you again!" asserted Margaret.

Owen shook his head. "All is not lost! Surely, you can believe there is something more pleasant than politics!"

"Pleasant? You are a Confederate!" retorted Margaret, her eyes brilliant, with conviction. "You represent everything I oppose! Everything that is rebellious, and wrong! Everything I am against! There can be nothing pleasant between us—-not now, or ever! And I promise I shall never think of you—-nor any pleasant diversion—-ever again!"

Margaret did not object however, when Owen caught her tightly, in his arms and kissed her. Nor was she at all amazed, when she returned the kiss—-not caring a whit for the silk ribbons which clung to Owen's rain-covered coat. It was only after the Captain departed that she remembered her duty to alert the Federal authorities. As she struggled to repair the shreds of her allegiance, Ginnie returned to the room.

"The May Belle has gone," she said, in voice devoid of spirit.

"Owen Ross, as well," Margaret replied. "He is a Confederate. You are are all Secessionists. I should go to the authorities at once!"

Ginnie could only close her eyes. Everything was falling to pieces.

The bell upon the shop door rang, and Mrs. Tarbox rushed in.

" 'E's comin'! An' 'e's got de' police!"

Ginnie knew immediately, who it was. Mr. Pike had not wasted time. And she had not expected him to.

The Federal agent burst into the room, and each rain-sodden footstep reverberated with menace. He was followed by Officer Magee, who carried a small length of rope.

Gideon Pike pointed to the young dressmaker. "That's the one. Take 'er, Magee!"

Ginnie fully expected the worst. All that was needed was her sister's accusation. And as Officer Magee approached with the rope, Margaret began to speak.

"Why, Mr. Pike! How superlative to see you, again! We were introduced during the Union Soiree!"

Gideon Pike squinted at Margaret.

"Miss MacGregor?" he asked, with palpable surprise.

"Indeed! Do you have any idea, that you are about to detain my sister?"

Ginnie was filled with astonishment. Especially when Margaret took her by the arm, and pulled her close.

"Your sister—-?" exclaimed Pike, his dark eyes losing their vicious luster.

"Really, Mr. Pike. I had thought Federal espionage a bit more reliable!"

"M-Miss MacGregor," sputtered Pike, "I have a Confederate letter. Found it on de' floor, in this very room!"

"A Confederate letter? Dear sir! Do you know how many ladies go in and out of the shop every day? Any number of them may have dropped it. The only thing the letter would prove, is that it was written by a Southern sympathizer."

Gideon Pike and his officer blinked at one another. Ida Tarbox backed against a wall, and barely breathed.

"You may be correct in that, Miss MacGregor," Pike finally stated, a trace of wariness in his voice. "We apologize for any disturbance. This misunderstanding shall be reported, immediately. Good day...ladies."

The two men quickly, departed. Gideon Pike however, sensed the familiar wisp of treason. Vigilance was needed. And Margaret MacGregor was a woman to be watched.

Seconds passed before anyone dared move or speak. Mrs. Tarbox separated herself from the wall, then gave Margaret a nod of admiration. "Thet sure was some fast talkin'! Whar de' heck're you from? Kentucky? Tennessee?"

"Massachusetts," replied Margaret.

"Massachusetts..." mused the farm lady. "Mus' be de' southern part."

The dressmaker had a more urgent question. "Those were the authorities. Whyever, did you protect me?"

The young woman from Boston, arched an eyebrow. "Is it not enough that you are my sister? And besides...I have detested Mr. Pike, since the moment we met."

Ginnie was speechless. Perhaps Margaret was not worthless, after all.

At that moment, Ida Tarbox decided to unfetter a fond desire. "Shore wish ah could blast thet Fed'ral agent from here ta perdition!"

Ginnie smiled at her most colorful patron. "I am grateful you took the risk to warn us of him."

"Ah jis' done what ah could. 'E's a bluebelly snake. An' we gotta git 'im, any way we kin!"

"And so, we shall," promised Ginnie. Someday. Somewhere. Somehow.

The farm lady departed, content that a cunning blow had been rendered for the South. Margaret, however, took on a more reflective manner...which was uncharacteristic at best, and troubling, at worst.

Ginnie straightened her collar. "And what is it, now?" she queried.

"I was deliberating upon our differences," said Margaret. "If we set them aside, we would definitely, have something in common."

"I see," replied Ginnie. "And might that—-"shared interest"—-be Captain Owen Ross?

Margaret looked her sister. How could she always divine the true meaning behind a cleverly-worded statement?

"You are going to marry him, are you not?" asked Ginnie.

Margaret hesitated. "Could—-would you mind?" she ventured, unsure of the reception for the general idea.

"Well, I wouldn't mind at all," declared her sister. "But I should be careful of what they have to say in Boston."

Margaret had not particularly, thought about that. But even if she were to bring a Confederate home, it would make little difference. Because now—-for Margaret Elizabeth MacGregor—-that no longer mattered.

Chapter Ten ~ The Last Farewell

Canon at the Ready

It was Sunday, June 26th, 1864...and the day before a battle. At a Union encampment outside Atlanta, Georgia, soldiers took their ease, or busied themselves with letters home. Laughter was heard among the small assemblies of men, who gathered to wile away time. The sunset that evening, gilded trees and woods...and from a small mountain, Confederate soldiers sang their Southern songs.

"Sit down, Guthrie. You make me jittery," said John Schiller, as he polished a well-used infantry bugle.

James Guthrie glanced from his binoculars. "That's four times those rebs've sung, "Dixie," he complained.

"Well, if they're singin', they ain't shootin,' " rationalized Schiller, buffing the brass with diligence.

Guthrie shook his head. "And the hardtack at dinner had bugs in it," he added.

"A regular complainer," observed Schiller, as he admired his reflection in the instrument. "I pitched mine."

Guthrie smiled. "Good for you, soldier!"

Schiller delayed, before further definition. "It crawled back," he said.

A warm breeze wafted as Lt. Charles Whittaker passed by. He noted the ethereal, blue of the summer sky, and the serenity that could not last.

'Evening, boys," he said, softly.

"Evening, Sir," offered Guthrie.

"Lt. Whittaker," added Schiller.

Charles took a deep breath of the early evening air. Whatever was to come on the morrow, would come. There was was only contentment in his soul at that moment.

"It has been a peaceful Sunday," he reflected.

"Very fine indeed, Sir," agreed Guthrie, hesitant to mention the rebel songs.

" 'Cept for the heat, mud, fleas, flies an' occasional, pot shot…it's been a real nice day, Lieutenant," admitted Schiller.

Guthrie turned his back on the mountain. "Is it true Colonel McCook's been chosen to lead, tomorrow?"

"It is," replied Charles. "We follow the Colonel."

Guthrie furrowed his brow. "Well, I've been watching the rebs, all day, Sir," he said, as he offered the binoculars to Charles. "They're sure dug in, up on that mountain."

Charles peered through the lenses. In the splendent sunset, the Confederate entrenchments were set aglow.

"They're dug in tight, Lieutenant," advised Schiller. "An' their musicality has beleaguered Guthrie here, all day."

"They sang "Dixie," four times, Sir!" asserted Guthrie, who much preferred anything but "Dixie."

"Aw, that was "The Bonnie Blue Flag," corrected Schiller. "He don' know many Southern ditties, Lieutenant."

"Their songs shall be the least of our worries tomorrow, boys," replied Charles, as he returned the lenses. He could only hope that General Johnston's line of men were indeed, stretched too thin.

"Has the Colonel received orders yet, Sir?" asked Guthrie, in a solemn tone.

"There has been a delay," replied Charles. "We shall have orders in the morning."

Guthrie nodded, and offered a strategy. "I'll wager we flank 'em! We've out-flanked Johnston, all over the map!"

"Flank 'em?" declared Schiller, "You see that line o' rebs, out there? Loring...Cheatham ...Hardee. Then there's Cleburne and Hood. We won't be flankin' 'em, this time!"

"What about the mountain?" retorted Guthrie. "You think General Sherman wants us to carry the works?"

"I know 'e does,"declared Schiller.

Guthrie shook his head. "But those Johnnies're too dug in—-"

Schiller stood, prepared to take on the argument. "An army's gotta fight, don' it? Grant's boys do."

"Grant's boys?" exclaimed Guthrie. "They don't fight—-they get slaughtered. My God..." James Guthrie looked directly at Charles. "Sir—-?" he asked. And it was more a plea, than a question.

Charles trained his eyes upon the mountain. Every man in McCook's Brigade would have to charge up its steep slope, among the entrenchments filled with Confederates. Eternity awaited many of those men. He turned to face Guthrie. There was never a good way to dull the sharp edge of truth.

"If General Sherman orders an attack...it shall be from the front."

Schiller contemplated those words. "Then Uncle Billy will have his fight...at Kennesaw Mountain."

For a time, each man became lost in thought. And each knew his chances of surviving a frontal attack.

Guthrie turned toward the sunset, and realized it might be the last he would ever see.

"Just look at that. "Reminds me of the poem Colonel McCook recites. How does that one part go, Lieutenant? The part about dying, I mean..."

Charles obliged, without hesitation.

"Then out spake brave Horatius, the Captain of the Gate: To every man upon this earth, death cometh soon or late. And how can man die nobler, when facing fearful odds...for the ashes of his fathers, and the temples of his gods."

John Schiller gripped the bugle, and held it aloft. In the waning light, it flashed with a bold brilliance.

"Well, we may be at de' sharp end o' de' fight...but de' 52nd Ohio Infantry stands ready! Goodnight, Lieutenant...Guthrie."

Charles gave a nod as Guthrie shook Schiller's hand. Then the bugler began his slow, lonely walk back to the line of soldiers' tents.

From a pocket, Guthrie withdrew a small, gilded case. He opened it and gazed upon the image within. "I have a girl, Lieutenant. Met her at the Tuscarawas County Fair. I talk to her sometimes...like she was here. Makes me feel better somehow." Guthrie closed the gilt-edged case. "Well, Sir...I bid you, goodnight."

"Goodnight, Private" said Charles.

Guthrie turned away, and Charles glimpsed the soldier's face. It was filled with the same desolation that had weighed for days, upon the Lieutenant. Charles' duty was to the Union. But he had begun to question the war he was fighting...and feared for what might be lost to him, forever.

As the private trudged away, Charles called out his name.

"Sir—-?" Guthrie queried, as he retraced his path.

Charles met him halfway, and extended his hand. "May all go well for you tomorrow, Private Guthrie."

James Guthrie reached out, and the men clasped hands. "And for you...Lt. Whittaker."

In the gathering twilight, Charles stood alone and watched the stars spangle the night. Life or death tomorrow, would depend upon the command of one Union General. And that General would send his troops forward, to charge up a mountainside filled with an enemy which was firmly entrenched. As the evening breeze began to stir, Charles thought of the only woman he had ever loved. Then he drew from his jacket a single, silk ribbon...the resplendent color of a summer sky.

Chapter Eleven ~ A Change of Plans

Mary Stuart Bonnet

Christmas Eve dawned cold and crisp, with window panes frosted, and glimmering in the winter light. At the shop on Verandah Row, the day was spent in Yuletide commerce. At mid-afternoon, the newly-widowed Mrs. Parmalee, sent over an envelope. Addressed to Ginnie, it contained a small memento from the late Mr. Parmalee, which the lady wished to pass along. Katie accepted the item, carefully placing it within her apron pocket. The day continued to be a cordial one. Then Mrs. Brumley entered the room. A red silk bonnet was required for the New Year.

"I shall expect the head-wear within three days," she ordered.

"But Mrs. Brumley," implored Katie, " 'tis Christmas Eve—-"

"I know which day it is! That bonnet shall be for New Years' visiting. And I shall have it within three days!"

The lady made a curt nod, and with a swirl of velvet, quickly departed. Katie shook her head, wishing she had closed the establishment much earlier. Then she thought of the dinner William had planned. As Ginnie and Mrs. Dawson arrived, Katie was humming a jaunty Irish tune, and lighting every candle and oil lamp in the shop.

"You seem exceedingly happy!" declared Mrs. Dawson, with a paper-wrapped package in her arms.

" 'Tis a special occasion!" smiled Katie, as she set another candle alight.

"Miss McCafferty shall be treated to dinner this evening," explained Ginnie, as she placed her package upon a shelf and took the other from the lady. "I do appreciate your assistance, Mrs. Dawson!"

The keys upon the lady's chatelaine gave a jingle. "It was a pleasure, Miss Allen! Oh, how fortunate you are, to have a shop on Verandah Row!"

"I am, indeed," agreed Ginnie. "Although, it seems constantly observed by the authorities."

"Thankfully, they do not keep watch upon our business," Mrs. Dawson replied. "And Captain Ross departs from there tonight, with the latest letters. He is to board the last ferry for Illinois."

Ginnie felt a vague uneasiness. "I just wish he would not be setting out on Christmas Eve..."

"Do not be distressed," pleaded the lady. "We have confounded the authorities. That abominable Federal agent has not one idea where to seek a single, Southern missive!"

"We ladies have been fortunate," admitted Ginnie, "But I feel something dreadful is about to happen."

"You needn't worry," soothed Mrs. Dawson. "All shall be well."

The lady wished everyone a "Happy Christmas," then took her leave. As Katie removed her pinner apron, she recalled Mrs. Parmalee's envelope.

"Holy angels—-I nearly forgot! Dis came from Mrs. Parmalee!"

While Katie chose a bonnet to wear, Ginnie placed the item within a drawer. As she did, the bell rang upon the shop door. Margaret entered, wearing a scarlet cloak over her gown, and was followed by William, splendidly attired in the finest of Boston tailoring.

"Margaret! Cousin Will—-!"

"Cousin Ginnie!" exclaimed William, as he removed his silk hat. "A vision of beauty, as always!"

"William has adopted Southern manners, of late," warned Margaret, removing her wrap.

"An agreeable modification, sir!" declared Ginnie.

"He now excels at flattery, as a duck at quacking," sniffed Margaret.

"I never use flattery, when the truth serves me better," testified William. "And as for quacking..."

Margaret glared at her cousin. St. Louis had certainly, been the worst of influences upon him.

"Well, I have been informed that two people shall be dining at the Planter's House!" smiled Ginnie, taking up a warm, woolen shawl for her milliner.

"Indeed!" said William as he gazed at Katie. "With no expense spared! I intend to return penniless!"

Margaret looked at her sister, and sighed. "Of course, our Christmas Eve shall be spent reading Dickens."

"Excellent choice in literature, Cousin!" agreed William. "Though a game of cards may be more to your liking."

Ginnie peered at William MacGregor. "Playing cards?" she asked, as she draped the shawl over Katie's shoulders.

"Indeed!" replied William. "Your father passed his prodigious knowledge of card games to your mother, which she dispensed quite liberally, to Margaret. I would never place a wager against your sister!" William turned, and offered his arm to Katie. "Shall we proceed to dinner, Miss McCafferty?"

Katie encircled his arm with hers, and the couple whisked away in a richly, furnished carriage. Then Ginnie awaited her sister's abysmal thoughts upon a well-worn subject.

"What a complete cataclysm!"asserted Margaret.

"Oh, sister," chided Ginnie. "Katherine McCafferty is a fine young lady—-"

"Shanty Irish!" decried Margaret. "I must consider the social impact!"

"You certainly must!" proclaimed Ginnie. "And perhaps also, ponder the impropriety of ladies who play at cards. Even if one of them was our mother!"

Margaret had no time to devise an answer. There was a knock upon the back door, and she hurried to unlatch it.

"Maggie—-!" said Owen as he entered the room, and each caught the other in a desperate embrace. Then Owen held out his hand to Ginnie.

"You should not have come here tonight!" she cautioned, as she kissed his cheek.

"I have information," announced Owen, his voice darkly, somber. "Cullie and Tom Donovan were at the Battle of Franklin. Their Brigade is decimated. Cullie survived the fight...Tom did not."

Ginnie's eyes burned, but she held back the tears. "Katie shall be grateful to know her brother still lives. Poor Tom...whatever shall his parents do? Oh, please, Owen—-please, be careful tonight!"

Owen nodded with a tight smile, and Margaret clung to him in a longing embrace. Upon his departure, Ginnie locked the door, while Margaret stood beside her, lost in desolation.

"I beg you not to cry," implored Ginnie, taking a handkerchief from her sleeve.

Margaret's eyes overflowed. "I am utterly helpless—-I shall die if he never returns!"

Ginnie placed an arm about her sister's shoulders. And although her own heart ached, she dabbed away Margaret's disconsolate tears.

"We must have confidence that all shall be well," she replied. "And be unrelenting in that belief."

The sisters promised to not be melancholy for Christmas. Then they busied themselves with a small dinner, enhanced by two festive glasses of Currant wine. With their spirits bolstered, they settled in for a quiet evening...far from the bustle of Yuletide, or the ghastly aspects of war. Then the bell upon the shop door rang.

Mrs. Tarbox entered, bearing a brightly colored basket. Something of obvious delight was inside.

"Happy Christmas, ladies!"

"Happy Christmas!" smiled Ginnie, as she rose to greet the lady.

Ida Tarbox gave a mirthful grin. "Jis' wanted ta bring ya somethin'! Lemme scrounge it up!" A gleaming glass jar was soon produced.

"Whatever is it?" asked Ginnie, holding the jar close to a lamp. "Why it's...pickles!"

"Had a ton o' cucumbers this year. Now we got a ton o' pickles!"

"Are they not good for digestion?" queried Margaret.

"De' best!" informed the farm lady. "So now you kin digest everthin' from bean fritters, ta fried pork sausage!"

The sisters were contemplating the gastronomic efficiency of the lowly pickle, when the shop door bell rang, with a seeming fury. In a blaze of color, Madam LaTour crossed the threshold.

"Madam—-!" exclaimed Ginnie.

Madam LaTour faced the women. "Ladies—-Captain Ross has been captured, boarding the ferry."

A cold shock ran through Ginnie. This was what she had feared all day.

Margaret MacGregor stared in distraught silence. The message had been delivered by a woman with whom she should not speak. It was simply not allowed in proper Boston society. But this was St. Louis—-and Margaret soon put words to each despairing thought.

"Where is he? Wherever is he being kept?"

"He is at City Jail," replied the Madam. "They are to hang him tomorrow."

Margaret grew pale, and the lady from Seventh Street gave her a quizzical look.

Ginnie hastily spoke up. "Madam LaTour—-I must introduce my sister, Margaret."

"You are Miss MacGregor?" asked the Madam, in surprise. "The one Captain Ross has spoken of?"

With Owen's life in peril, Margaret no longer had need of proper decorum.

"Please, Madam LaTour," she pleaded." We must do something, swiftly!"

"Yes, we must," answered the Madam. "But first we need a plan. And a good one."

The sisters wrapped their arms about each other, and four women contemplated the release a condemned man from City Jail. Some way, it had to be done. And be done that very night.

Ida Tarbox offered the first idea. "Ah kin pick a lock. Do it all de' time at de' back pasture."

"You shall have to wear mens' clothing..." emphasized Madam LaTour.

"Thet's no problem," admitted the farm lady, as she withdrew a corncob pipe.

Ginnie's notion was next. "I shall purchase two train tickets for Boston!" she declared. And having heard of the card games at City Jail, said twelve words she never thought would pass her lips.

"You must wager at cards this evening, Margaret. And you must win."

Margaret looked from her sister to the Madam, who had pieced the plan together.

"The Officers at City Jail favor 'Draw Poker.' Do you know the game?"

A stealthy smile crept across Margaret's face. "Madam LaTour," she said, "we have a plan!"

As the sisters made their farewells, both realized it could be months—-or years—-before one would see the other. And each knew what a terrible risk was about to be undertaken.

"I am afraid I shan't see you for quite a while," said Ginnie, as tears finally, began to fall.

Margaret nodded, her own cheeks deluged. "Promise you'll come to Boston. Promise!"

Ginnie agreed, although it meant the closing of the shop. It was time to return to her family. If only she had heard from Charles, but there was too much danger in their correspondence. The sisters embraced one last time, then Margaret followed the ladies out into the winter night.

As Ginnie began to put out the lamps, she remembered Mrs. Parmalee's envelope, and gently, retrieved it from the drawer. The inscription noted its contents had come from the battlefield at Kennesaw Mountain, Georgia, and bore the date of June 27th, 1864. Whatever it contained was a personal memento from the battle. Ginnie slowly opened the envelope, and the item inside, fell like a whisper into her hand. As it did, she caught her breath. For there in the candlelight, like an unfulfilled promise, was a solitary ribbon...the color of a summer sky.

Chapter Twelve ~ The Wagering Game

Gratiot Street Prison

City Jail was awash in celebratory light. The gray, grim interior was lit by several oil lamps, and a wood stove cast a comforting glow from a corner. The reason for the euphoric mood, was the long-anticipated capture—-and death upon the morrow—-of a Confederate mail-runner. And though known for his taciturn disposition, no one was more pleased, than Gideon Pike.

"Well, boys," he gloated, as he extracted a cigar from his coat, "Captain Owen Ross is ours!"

"Aye, Mr. Pike! agreed Officer Flann O'Malley.

"You hang 'im good, O'Malley!" directed Pike, as he struck a match. "It took long enough ta catch 'im!"

"Then ya'll not be stayin' fer de' hangin'?" asked Officer Michael Magee, as he warmed his hands at the stove.

Gideon Pike gave an unusually blissful, one-sided smile. "Business, boys! I'm bound fer Chicago!"

"We'll have a grand time fer ya, then," promised O'Malley, seating himself at a spare, wooden table.

"De' bes' ta be had!" declared Officer Paddy Hannigan, his boyish face enhanced by a smile.

"I trust it shall be so," said Pike, as he took a puff on the cigar. "And be watchful, tonight, boys. Watchful!"

"We will, Sir," pledged Magee. "We will, indeed!"

Assured the demise of Owen Ross was well in hand, Gideon Pike felt confidant to leave the city. He had done his best in St. Louis. But when a departure of this sort was being made, one must leave with a stringent reminder.

"Good-bye, then. An' never forget, boys—vigilance! Vigilance. Yer no good to de' Union, without it!"

The Federal agent stepped into the crackling night air, as three women watched, in silent secrecy. And when he was safely from view, the ladies put their plan for the evening into devastating action.

Madam LaTour and Margaret stepped onto the cold stone floor of City Jail. "Good evening, gentlemen," smiled the Madam, as she motioned to Margaret. "We hope you will not mind a convivial holiday visit."

"Madam LaTour!" smiled O'Malley. "Not at all. We were havin' a genial eve'nin', ourselves."

"Aye," agreed Magee, pulling out a chair. "We've a hangin' in de' mornin', so we're celebratin' a bit early!"

The Madam fanned, with a languid grace. "On Christmas Day? Do the City Police never rest?"

" 'Tis our duty!" exclaimed O'Malley.

"An' we keep strictly ta regulations," asserted Magee, as he seated himself upon the chair.

"Besides," explained Hannigan, "de' man's a rebel. 'Tis best we hang 'im sooner, than later!"

"I see!" declared Madam LaTour. "Such efficiency! One hardly needs the Chief of Police!"

"Thank all that's holy," nodded Hannigan, as he sat upon a chair.

Magee shook his head. "If de' Chief was here, we'd be playin' 'Checkers,'as we should."

Officer Flann O'Malley withdrew a fresh deck of playing cards from his pocket.

"But since 'e's not," he grinned, "we kin have a nice, civilized game o' Poker!"

"A wagering game!" proclaimed Margaret, with an air of pleased astonishment.

The Officers looked with curiosity, upon the Madam's companion. Her curled hair and painted face imparted a doll-like appearance, and the flamboyant gown—-with glittering gewgaws—-increased the effect, considerably.

"Gentlemen," said Madam LaTour, "this—-is Miss Marguerite!"

Officer Magee, as Head Official at City Jail, was first to complete the introductions.

"Miss Marguerite—-I'm Officer Magee. Dis here's Hannigan...an' dere's O'Malley!

"A pleasure, gentlemen!" enthused Margaret.

"D'ya play cards, Miss?" ventured Hannigan, a smile playing over his blue-eyed face.

Margaret was hesitant. "Oh—-just a little..."

"Well, Magee...a fourth player might prove amusin'," smirked O'Malley, as he placed the cards upon the table.

Magee frowned. "Vigilance, O'Malley. Vigilance.

"Sorry, Miss," shrugged Hannigan. " 'Tis regulations."

"Well, I do possess several coins," responded Margaret, with a jingle of the reticule she wore upon her wrist.

O'Malley looked up. "Silver—?"

Margaret nodded. "Several half-dimes and a quarter!"

"Union men are so very generous," noted the Madam with a languorous, wave of the effulgent fan.

O'Malley and Hannigan looked at one another, then at the Head Official.

"All right, then," sighed Magee, "Clear a space."

With their thoughts set upon winning the coins, a fourth chair was added, and Margaret chose to sit facing the Madam. In the rush to be seated, no one noticed a small figure in mens' clothing enter the room. Nor did they see Madam LaTour direct that figure with her fan, to the jail cells at the rear. When all were seated, Margaret placed her coin-laden reticule upon the table. Then she looked up at Madam LaTour, who nodded once, and slowly fanned.

"Now, then...d'ya know much about cards, Miss Marguerite?" inquired O'Malley.

"Nothing to mention," replied Margaret, as the Madam hid a smile behind a swath of crimson feathers.

O'Malley winked. "Well, no man's ever beaten Flann O'Malley at dis game—-so 'Draw Poker' it is!"

Hannigan gave Margaret a sheepish look. "We boys have no silver...only paper currency, I'm afraid."

"Federal paper currency?" smiled Margaret. "Surely as good as coin, gentlemen!" To prove her conviction, a silver half-dime was placed upon the table. It glimmered in the lamplight.

"A silver piece..." breathed Magee.

"Ain't it pretty," sighed Hannigan.

"I'll be winnin' that from ya, Miss!" vowed O'Malley.

Each placed their bets. O'Malley shuffled the cards. Magee cut the deck. The deal was made, and the players viewed the cards within their hand.

"Yer bet, Miss Marguerite..." directed O'Malley.

"I believe I shall wager fifteen cents." Three silver coins soon shimmered upon the tabletop.

"I call," said Hannigan.

"I call, as well," said Magee.

"I call, an' dere's mine," said O'Malley. "How many, Miss?"

"One, please," replied Margaret, as she placed a card upon the table.

"Hannigan?" queried O'Malley.

Hannigan discarded, as well. "Gimme two," he said.

"What'll it be, Magee?" asked O'Malley.

Officer Magee placed most of his cards upon the table. "I'll take three..."

O'Malley dealt three cards, then checked his own hand. He discarded, and drew two. After a pause, Margaret felt the intensity of his eyes.

"Yer bet, Miss," he advised, tapping his cards upon the table.

Margaret smiled. "I shall wager a quarter dollar." Soon, another silver coin scintillated in the lamplight.

"I call," said Hannigan.

"I, as well," said Magee.

All had placed their bets, except Officer O'Malley.

"I call...an' raise fifty cents."

Madam LaTour ceased to fan, with her intensely-colored accessory. Every eye was upon Margaret.

"I shall see your wager, sir. And raise one dollar. In silver."

Magee and Hannigan did not ponder their strategy.

"I'm out...thank de' Saints!" proclaimed Hannigan.

Magee did the same, and took a silent vow to never again, play a card game.

Officer O'Malley studied Margaret's face. Her expression was undecipherable. She played the game with an easy coolness...an aptitude he had observed only in men. No female played at cards that way unless she was well-schooled, or oblivious. He reckoned it must be the latter. After all...Miss Marguerite was only a woman.

"Well, then! The game is ours, Miss Marguerite! I'll see yer wager, an' raise two dollars. Now...what shall it be?"

The Madam primped the brilliant feathers upon her fan, as Margaret took several coins from her reticle.

"I shall see that, Officer O'Malley. And raise five dollars. In gold."

Nothing seemed to stir in the hush that followed. Each gold coin made a light, clear jingle as it was placed upon the silver. And while the Officers were enthralled by the sight and sound, Owen Ross made his escape with the dapperly dressed, Mrs. Tarbox.

"Have I not played the game properly?" inquired Margaret.

"Indeed, you have!" beamed O'Malley, as he placed his cards face-up. "I've a Full House!"

" A Full House!" declared Hannigan."

"No man beats Flann O'Malley," intoned Magee, shaking his head over the man, as well as the game.

"Well, Miss Marguerite," smiled O'Malley, "whattaya have, then?"

Margaret pondered her cards. "Oh, Officer...I am afraid I have only nines."

With a victorious grin, O'Malley began to gather up the gleaming coins. "Nines? Well, ya'd be needin' two pair of 'em ta beat my hand!"

Margaret placed five cards face-up, upon the table. Two pairs of nines lay side by side.

"Sweet Glory o' Heaven—-!" exclaimed Hannigan.

" 'Tis Four of a Kind," marveled Magee.

"You should be proud, Miss Marguerite," congratulated the Madam. "It was a game, fairly won!"

A cloud of anger skittered across O'Malley's face. "Fairly won? She played like a bandit!"

Hannigan gave a hearty laugh. "Ya've been picked clean!" he declared. " Like a Tom turkey!"

" 'Twas a fancy man that taught 'er de' game," advised Magee. "No doubt about it."

O'Malley simmered with bitterness. How could he have been bested by a trollop? Of course, a man had taught her the game! There were fancy men everywhere. And whoever he was—-he was one Ace of a card player.

"Who was de' scurrilous scoundrel?" raged O'Malley.

Margaret collected the currency littering the table. "Scoundrel? Of which scoundrel, do you speak?"

" 'Tis a secret, then, who taught ya de' game?" pursued the Officer.

Margaret stood, then gave a charming smile. "It is no secret, sir. It has never been."

O'Malley's face began to redden. "Then who, under almighty heaven, was de' blighted bounder?"

Margaret fixed her gaze fully, upon Officer Flann O'Malley.

"Why, sir," she said, with proper Bostonian propriety, "the 'blighted bounder' was...my mother!"

Epilogue ~ Taking Leave

Woman in Mirror

In April of 1865 the Civil War ended. It was now the month of June, and Ginnie had closed her shop. A different establishment would very soon take its place.

The bell upon the shop door rang, and Ginnie stepped into the empty room. She was followed by Mrs. Dawson, the new proprietress of the property.

"I hope the room shall be to your liking," said Ginnie.

Mrs. Dawson looked about, with awe. "I have been awaiting a fashionable address for years! But are you certain, Miss Allen—-?"

For Ginnie, there was only one answer. "Here are the keys. I am quite certain."

The lady accepted the brass items, and placed them upon her chatelaine. "Thank you, Miss Allen. I shall endeavor to make this room as successful as it has ever been!"

Ginnie's face brightened. "Have you an idea for your emporium?"

Mrs. Dawson smiled. "It shall be a shop for fancy goods—gilded combs, glass buttons, artificial flowers...all manner of beautiful things! And I have ordered perfume—-all the way from Cincinnati!"

"Perfume!" declared Ginnie. "You shall certainly, outdo yourself!"

"Oh, I have many plans...but how I wish you would not leave us. Boston is so different a place—-"

"It is, "agreed Ginnie, "but I must keep a promise to my sister."

Mrs. Dawson nodded. "I understand. It is the proper thing to do."

The bell rang upon the shop door, and Ida Tarbox entered the room.

"Mornin' all!" she exclaimed, richly clothed in a striped dress, enhanced by a straw bonnet with an ostrich plume. Though an unredeemed Confederate, the farm lady had acquired a fashion sense to rival that of any French couturier.

Ginnie smiled at the visitor, who now wore fine leather shoes.

Mrs. Tarbox has consented to be my saleslady," apprised Mrs. Dawson. "Mrs. Parmalee, as well...though she is still in deep mourning."

"Three more months in black bombazine." elaborated Ida Tarbox, with little affection, for the afflicted fabric.

Mrs. Dawson was quick to change the subject. "And the women's suffrage movement has our undivided attention! It is high time women gained the right to vote. Even if it takes half a century!"

"Prob'ly longer," mused Mrs. Tarbox.

Ginnie was amazed at the wonders taking place. Ladies...choosing to be employed? Women... gaining the vote? "I am departing, when everything is beginning!"

Mrs. Dawson gave a tender smile. "Do not forget...you also, are making a new beginning!"

The bell upon the shop door gave a sprightly jingle, and Madam LaTour stepped into the room. She sported a muslin gown with a blue silk vest, and a white straw hat, trimmed with peacock feathers. A lace fan dangled from her wrist.

"Well—-ladies!" she said, with a graceful curtsy.

"Oh!" exclaimed Mrs. Dawson, who never quite knew how to react to the demimonde.

"Mornin', Madam!" said the farm lady. "Ah shore like them peacock tails on yer head!"

Madam LaTour nodded, graciously.

Ginnie held out her hands to the lady from Seventh Street. She knew this parting was to be their last.

The Madam took Ginnie's hands in hers. "My dear, Miss Allen! I could not let you depart without my appreciative, farewell. Is it Boston, then?"

"It is, indeed," affirmed Ginnie. "My sister—-"

"Ah! Your sister," declared Madam LaTour. "Married five months to Captain Ross! A lady of neglected talent and unlimited, possibilities. You shall both be missed. A happy life, Miss Allen."

Ginnie gave a grateful smile to the woman who had become such an important part of her life. "And, to you as well...Madam LaTour."

The lady from Seventh Street nodded, then swept around to face the other women. She made an elegant bow.

"Ladies...my compliments. And Mrs. Dawson—-my girls and I look forward to visiting your new establishment. I have heard you shall have perfume!"

Mrs. Dawson gave a tentative smile, while Mrs. Tarbox made a mental note of the peacock-feather hat. Then the Madam removed the fan from her wrist, and placed it within Ginnie's hands.

"For your sister," she said with an evanescent smile. Then amidst a flutter of fine muslin, she was gone.

Mrs. Dawson gave Ida Tarbox a look of unsullied trepidation.

"Oh, don' worry 'bout them gals," advised farm lady. "They'll only stop by a few times each week!"

Ginnie stood at the display window, and looked out onto Fourth Street. The sights, the smells, the ever present cacophony, the mixture of colors and the incessant, bustle of St. Louis...all were to be left far behind.

The bell rang upon the shop door, and Katie entered the room.

"I'm here ta collect Miss Ginnie," she said.

Though married but two months to William, Katie looked every bit the young society wife. Mrs. Dawson smiled. "Mrs. MacGregor! You are the exact replica of a Godey's fashion plate!"

Katie twirled about for all to see. Her new husband cared nothing for the cost of her equipage. And all the better. Her new ensemble was of the uppermost fashion. And the costliest price.

Mrs. Tarbox cast a discerning eye upon the lavish apparel. "Busted buckets! Thet's six yards of Irish silk poplin!"

Though deeply sorrowful, Ginnie suppressed a smile. No one could replace Ida Tarbox. Then with a reluctant sigh, she turned toward Katie. "Is it time?" she asked.

"Almost," the new Mrs. MacGregor, replied. "De' train leaves in thirty minutes."

Mrs. Dawson shook her head, and Mrs. Tarbox invoked the recent past. "Jis' remember how we hornswoggled 'em at City Jail. Thet snake-eyed cuss is prob'ly still confounded!"

"We had the perfect plan," said Ginnie. "Oh, how I shall miss you, both."

Mrs. Dawson's chin began to tremble. "Come now, Ida...before I commence to cry."

The ladies took their leave, and stepped into the overwhelming brightness of a summer morning. For the women of St. Louis, life had changed...never to be the same, again.

In the empty room, Katie stood quietly, and interlaced her fingers. Some startling information was about to be liberally, divulged.

"Dere's somethin' I have ta tell ya. Cullie is comin' with us."

"You—-your brother?" stammered Ginnie.

" 'E arrived on a steamer, yesterday! It took some doin'...but William talked 'im into bein' on de' Base Ball team!"

Ginnie was astounded. Boston, Massachusetts, was about to inherit two Confederates.

Katie's face dimpled. "Ev'rythin' has worked out perfectly! Now all we need do is board de' train!"

Ginnie smiled for Katie's sake, though her own life was filled with a sad imperfection. "Please..." she begged, "let me have just a moment longer."

Katie stepped onto Fourth Street, and gently closed the door behind her. For one last time, the dressmaker looked about the room. So much of her life had been lived within its walls...and now, they belonged to someone else. She placed her fingertips to her collar, and felt the blue silk ribbon at her throat. It was always, with her now. And though many recollections whirled about, there was only one memory she would cherish, forever.

"Dear, Charles," she said, as softly a prayer, "it seems a lifetime since I saw you last. I suppose it was always to end like this. But I wish I could tell you, what I should have always known. That there can be nothing more precious to hope for in this world, than someone's love. And if love be lost...then may the wonder of it, never cease." As she buried her face in her hands, the bell upon the shop door rang.

For an instant, Ginnie dared not move, and her heart beat, wildly. Then footsteps echoed in the stillness. Might Gideon Pike have returned? With nothing more than a fervent hope, she trembled in the free-fall of an endless moment—-only to be saved by a destiny, too long delayed. "Ginnie, my love," said a familiar voice, and she caught her breath. Then with a soft, sweep of fabric she turned...and ran to the waiting arms of her Lieutenant.

Illustrations and Credits

Cover: Portion of period woodblock engraving of couple dancing (see Chapter 7) framed by part of first Confederate national flag.

Prologue: "St. Louis Levee or Landing" 1857 illustration from *Ballou's Pictorial Drawing Room Companion*, Boston.

Chapter 1: "Verandah Row, Fourth Street" Between Washington and St. Charles.

Cut from page 169 of *"Ballou's Pictorial Drawing-Room Companion"*-1857.

Chapter 2: "Lady in Feather Hat" Spring robe of pearl-colored cambric stamped to represent back braiding from *Godey's Lady's Books, April 1865*.

Chapter 3: "Man with beard in Evening Attire" likely from *Godey's Lady's Books*.

Chapter 4: "Brown leghorn straw hat with full brown feather and black velvet ribbon" from *Godey's Lady's Books,* July 1861.

Chapter 5: "Planter's House Hotel on Fourth Street" Horizontal wood engraving from *Frank Leslie's Illustrated Newspaper*, June 13, 1857.

Chapter 6: "Two Women wearing Day Look" hand colored. Artist unknown. *Englishwoman's Domestic Magazine*, Tuesday, March 1, 1864. Los Angeles:

Chapter 7: "A Cadet Hop at West Point", 1859. Based on sketch by Winslow Homer Wood engraving. Published *Harpers Weekly*, September 3, 1859.

Chapter 8: "Birdcage Hoop Skirt" by Douglas & Sherwood's New Expansion Skirt

from *Godey's Lady's Book*, May 1858.

Chapter 9: "Straw Hat with Flowers"from *Godey's Lady's Book May 1865*.

Chapter 10: "Canon at the Ready" photographed by author at Jerseyville Illinois Rendezvous.

Chapter 11: "Mary Stuart Bonnet" likely from *Godey's Lady's Books*

Chapter 12: Wood engraving after oil painting of McDowell's Medical College as the *Gratiot Street Prison* by Martin Stadler during the Civil War. A Federal prison located at 8th and Gratiot Streets, held prisoners of all types who had been accused of committing crimes—civilians, spies, guerrillas and even Federal soldiers—not just Confederate prisoners of war.

Epilogue: "Woman in Mirror" *Godey's Lady's Book and Magazine* - Vols. 52 and 53.

About the Author

Monika L. Burkhart became fascinated by Missouri's Civil War history, especial how it affected Saint Louis. She began researching this history through letters, journals and newspaper accounts at the **Missouri Historical Society Library & Archives**. Many of the documents were on microfilm. There were only a limited number of microfilm machines with copying, and she felt bad about dominating their use. Though a generous donation, company match and funds from the Missouri Historical Society another machine was bought. It is still in use today.

Her writings have been published in local and regional magazines. Other interests include graphic art and evocative wall decor photography. Many of her images are available though on-line retailers.

Read more at www.lupabox.com.